MOUSE NOSES
ON TOAST

MOUSE NOSES ON TOAST

Daren King

Illustrated by
David
Roberts

MOUSE
NOSES
SMELL

HANDS
F OUR
OSES

SAVE
OUR
NOSES

SAVE
OUR
NOSES

JUST
because
we SQUEAK
doesn't mean
we're MEEK

ff

faber and faber

First published in 2006
by Faber and Faber Limited
3 Queen Square London WC1N 3AU

Design by Mandy Norman
Printed in England by Mackays of Chatham Plc,
Chatham, Kent

A CIP record for this book
is available from the British Library

ISBN 978-0-571-22802-7
ISBN 0-571-22802-X

2 4 6 8 10 9 7 5 3 1

To Kevin Conroy Scott

CONTENTS

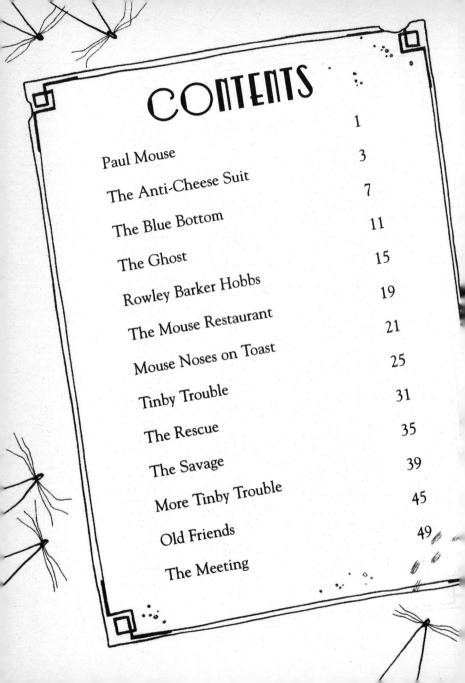

PAUL MOUSE

IN A BUSY TOURIST TOWN LIVED A MOUSE NAMED PAUL.

Most mouses are friends with other mouses. Paul was an unusual mouse, not just because he was in a story, but because his friends were a variety of animals, creatures and objects.

One of his friends was a Tinby, which is a sort of monster, though smaller than a monster and a lot more fun to be around. Like all Tinbys, it was curved at the top and flat at the bottom, with little square legs, tiny black eyes, and nothing else. It was yellow and patterned with lime-green checks.

If you are wondering why a Tinby is called a Tinby, you will find out later in the story, when the Tinby falls out of a window and makes a funny sound.

Another of Paul's friends was a Christmas-tree decoration, a plastic angel named Sandra who had been brought to life by a magician in another story.

Paul, Sandra and the Tinby lived in a cardboard shoebox at the bottom of an overgrown garden. They didn't know who owned the garden, but whoever it was had a dog named Rowley Barker Hobbs, who would run out into the garden every day and say hello.

Rowley Barker Hobbs was a shaggy sheepdog, with a hairy head at one end and a busy tail at the other. If the head was happy the tail was happier, and wagged all day long to prove it.

THE ANTI-CHEESE SUIT

PAUL DID HAVE SOME MOUSE FRIENDS, BUT HE DIDN'T SEE them often because he was allergic to cheese, and the mouses ate cheese all day long.

Whenever Paul wanted to visit his mouse friends he had to wear a special suit called an anti-cheese suit. If he stood too close to some cheese without the suit, his bottom would turn blue, the fur would fall out and his tail would curl up like a question mark.

Paul had made the suit himself out of clingfilm. You and I know that clingfilm is a type of clear plastic for wrapping sandwiches. Paul knew this too, but the other mouses didn't. Whenever they saw him in the suit they thought he was wearing the height of mouse fashion.

'Nice suit, Paul,' the mouses would say when he arrived.

'Thanks,' he would reply, brushing himself down. The mouses lived under the floorboards in the storeroom of a restaurant, and the storeroom was always dusty.

Paul Mouse would look around at all the happy

mouses, sat in cheesy chairs, eating cheese and watching Cheddar Television, and wish that he was not allergic to cheese.

On Paul's most recent visit, one morning in high summer, Graham Mouse asked Paul Mouse why he always sat on the floor.

'There aren't enough chairs,' Paul said. He didn't want to tell the mouses about his allergy. They might laugh. Who ever heard of a mouse allergic to cheese?

'You can have my chair,' Graham Mouse said, standing up. 'I'm off to the mouse pub for a pint of Old Stilton beer.'

Paul frowned. If he sat in the cheesy chair, his bottom would turn blue, the fur would fall out and his tail would curl up like a question mark.

'You'd better sit in the chair,' one of the mouses said, 'or Graham will be offended.'

Paul had always been afraid of Graham Mouse. He was a big, burly mouse with the words LIKE and HATE tattooed across his paws.

Graham Mouse put on his denim jacket, the one he wore when he felt like punching someone on the whiskers, and said, 'Paul, do you want my chair or not?'

Paul looked at the cheesy chair, then up at Graham's mean face, then back at the cheesy chair. How bad could it be? After all, he was wearing the anti-cheese suit.

So Paul Mouse sat on the cheesy chair.

Later, when none of the other mouses were looking, Paul stood up and peered at his bottom in a mirror. It was blue, and completely bald.

THE BLUE BOTTOM

SOMEHOW, PAUL MANAGED TO slip out of the mousehole without the other mouses seeing his bottom. The scamper home was more difficult. A lady mouse called him a blue-bottomed maniac. He was chased by a policemouse and laughed at by a group of teenage rats smoking cigarettes.

In the overgrown garden, Rowley Barker Hobbs was running round in circles, barking at himself and chasing his tail. 'Hello,' he said, when Paul Mouse stepped out from behind a tuft of grass.

'Rowley Barker Hobbs, if only I had bumped into you an hour ago,' Paul said. 'You could have given me a ride home.'

'Sorry about that,' Rowley Barker Hobbs said, poking out his pink tongue. 'What happened to your bottom?'

'The anti-cheese suit was supposed to protect it,' Paul said, tearing off the suit and stamping it into the mud.

'I like cheese,' Rowley Barker Hobbs said. 'I buried one just this morning.'

'You're thinking of bones,' Paul said. 'You always get cheese and bones muddled up. Cheese is yellow and smelly, and it makes my bottom turn blue.'

Rowley Barker Hobbs nodded his big shaggy head. 'I have to go now,' he said, 'but I will come and say hello again tomorrow.' And he ran in through the back door of the house.

Paul Mouse made his way to the end of the garden. It had rained recently and the shoebox was sopping wet. Sandra was trying to dry it by wiping it with a huge tissue. For a plastic Christmas-tree decoration, Sandra was very houseproud.

'Where did you get the tissue?' Paul asked.

'The Tinby borrowed a whole box from the supermarket,' Sandra replied, pretending not to have noticed Paul's blue bottom.

Paul was impressed. How the Tinby had carried the box home with no arms was a mystery. He gave the

Tinby a thumbs-up. The Tinby bowed its curved top half, but said nothing.

'Have you been to see the mouses at the restaurant?' Sandra asked.

'Yes,' Paul said, 'and while I was there, something terrible happened.' He turned round and bent over.

'Your poor bottom!'

'I will never go to that restaurant again,' Paul said, trying to straighten out his question-mark-shaped tail.

Sandra thought.

The Tinby thought too, but no one knew what it was thinking as Tinbys think in colours and shapes.

'I have an idea,' Sandra said. 'I think you should go to the restaurant one more time, not to see the mouses but for a posh meal. You deserve it after what you've been through.'

Paul smiled. He liked this idea a lot.

'We can go today,' Sandra said. 'You, me, the Tinby and Rowley Barker Hobbs.'

THE GHOST

PAUL, SANDRA AND THE TINBY SPENT THE REST OF THE morning drying the shoebox with tissues. No one likes to return home to a soggy shoebox.

When they had made the shoebox as dry as they could, they lifted the lid and climbed inside. It was time to get ready for their posh meal.

Sandra took the longest to get ready as she had to choose a dress. She only had one dress and was already wearing it, but she took a long time to choose it anyway as she wanted to look her best.

The Tinby didn't wear clothes, so Paul drew a bow tie on its front, just below the eyes, with a black felt-tip pen. 'Shall I colour it in?'

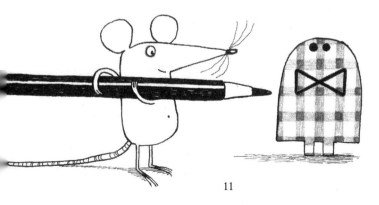

'No,' Sandra said, 'it would look too formal.'

Paul left the bow tie as it was, yellow with lime-green checks.

In return for the bow tie, the Tinby made Paul an elegant cape out of tissue, and Sandra found an acorn and carved it into a posh acorn hat.

And finally, they were ready. They climbed out of the shoebox and went to knock for Rowley Barker Hobbs.

When they reached the house, they half expected Rowley Barker Hobbs to come bouncing out through the back door, wagging his tail and saying hello. But Rowley Barker Hobbs only came out once a day, and he had said hello once today already.

'We could knock for him,' Paul said.

Sandra put her hand on her silver hip. 'You do the knocking, Paul Mouse. I'm an angel, and knocking is not very angelic.'

So Paul knocked on the wood with his paw.

They waited and waited and waited, but the door did not open and Rowley Barker Hobbs did not come out and say hello.

'We could shout his name,' Paul said. 'He will hear

us if we all shout together.'

'The Tinby can't shout, Paul. It hasn't got a mouth.'

'Where is the Tinby anyway?'

The Tinby was doing something daring. It had climbed up the outside of the back door and was jumping up and down on the door handle, with no arms and no regard for its own safety.

'I hope it doesn't fall,' Sandra said, almost in tears.

'Me too,' Paul said. 'We don't want broken Tinby bits all over the patio.'

Suddenly, the door handle turned and the door swung open. Paul and Sandra climbed up the doorstep and walked into the house.

'The carpet looks hot,' Paul said. It was mauve and patterned with fiery orange swirls.

'I don't like it,' Sandra said. 'My wings are made of tinsel, and tinsel is highly flammable.'

'I hope we don't get carpet burns,' Paul said. 'It is warm in here. I may have to take off my hat.'

They kept close to the wall in case there were humans wearing boots, but something far worse than boots awaited them. In the centre of the room, crouched on the fiery carpet, was a huge white ghost.

Paul hid behind Sandra and Sandra hid behind Paul.

'Look at its eyes,' Paul said. 'Rowley Barker Hobbs has eyes like that.'

'Maybe it is Rowley Barker Hobbs,' Sandra said. 'He might have died and turned into a ghost.'

This was a horrible thought, but it was too late. The thought had been thought.

'Get a bit closer,' Paul said, 'and ask it its name.'

Sandra took several steps forward, so that she was almost close enough to smell the ghost's ghostly breath. 'Is your name Rowley?'

The ghost shook its head.

Sandra turned and ran, more scared than she had ever been in her life.

ROWLEY BARKER HOBBS

PAUL DIDN'T RUN. HE MARCHED RIGHT UP TO THE GHOST, so close he really could smell its ghostly breath, which actually smelt more like dog food, and asked the ghost if its name was Rowley Barker Hobbs.

The ghost nodded, reached out a hairy paw, and pulled the white blanket from its shaggy head.

'We thought you were a ghost,' Paul said.

Rowley Barker Hobbs looked down at the ghostly blanket, gave it a playful bite.

Sandra came back from where she was hiding, behind a chair leg. 'I asked if your name was Rowley and you shook your head.'

'His name isn't Rowley,' Paul said. 'It's Rowley Barker Hobbs. Isn't that right, Rowley Barker Hobbs?'

Rowley Barker Hobbs nodded, barked a hello, and ran round in a circle, catching the tip of his tail between his teeth.

'I like your hat,' Rowley Barker Hobbs said when he had finished chasing his tail.

'Thank you,' Paul said handsomely. 'We're off to a

restaurant. Will you come?'

'I only go out once a day,' Rowley Barker Hobbs said, 'and I've been out once today already.'

'You could go out twice today,' Sandra said, 'and stay in all day tomorrow.'

Rowley Barker Hobbs thought about this. He thought about a today with two Rowley Barker Hobbs in it and a tomorrow with no Rowley Barker Hobbs in it. Then he thought about a restaurant with a bone in it, and a Rowley Barker Hobbs who licked the bone until it shone.

Back outside, the Tinby was still on the door handle. When it saw its three friends, it dropped off the door handle and landed on the patio with a heavy thud.

'Oh dear,' Sandra said, wiping an angelic tear from her eye. 'I hope it isn't broken.'

But Tinbys are made of tough stuff. Perhaps this is why they are so brave.

Rowley Barker Hobbs crouched down so that Paul, Sandra and the Tinby could climb onto his back. He pushed open the garden gate with his padded nose and padded out into the street.

'I hope you know the way,' Paul said, lifting a

shaggy ear.

Rowley Barker Hobbs shook his head. 'I thought I would follow my tummy.'

'Don't worry, Paul,' Sandra said. 'We seem to be going in the right direction. If he takes a wrong turn, the Tinby can tug his tail.'

Somehow, Rowley Barker Hobbs delivered them directly to the restaurant door. And this was where they met their next problem. A sign on the door read: NO DOGS.

'You have to wait out here, Rowley Barker Hobbs,' Sandra said.

'What about my tummy? Does my tummy have to wait out here too?'

'I'm afraid it does,' Sandra said. 'The Tinby will bring you a bone from the kitchen.'

THE MOUSE RESTAURANT

THE DOOR WAS MADE OF VERY OLD WOOD, AND HAD A tiny crack in one corner.

Paul squeezed through first, followed by the Tinby and then Sandra, who removed her tinsel halo to prevent it from breaking. The tip of Rowley Barker Hobbs' nose poked through too, to say hello.

'The mouses live out the back,' Paul said, pointing towards the dusty storeroom.

'Forget the mouses,' Sandra said. 'Let's eat!'

The Mouse Restaurant was by the far wall of the human restaurant, under a charming antique dresser. To reach it, you had to cross an area of polished stone tiles and weave between the chair legs and table legs of the dining table without getting squished.

They were lucky to get a table. The Mouse Restaurant had recently been awarded Five Golden Cheeses in *Mouse About Town* magazine, and was packed with fashionable rodents from all over the country. Fortunately, the mouse waiter mistook the Tinby for a famous film star, and offered them a table reserved for the Mouse Mayor.

'We should order a bottle of wine,' Sandra said. 'It's not a posh meal without wine.'

'A bottle of mouse red,' Paul told the mouse waiter.

'Certainly, sir,' the waiter said, and disappeared through a hole in the skirting board.

'I don't know what to have,' Sandra said as they studied the menu.

They were still choosing when the waiter came back with the wine, so Paul straightened his acorn hat and asked the waiter to recommend something.

'The breadcrumbs are fresh today,' the waiter said, scratching his whiskers. 'We also have a squashed sausage.'

'That doesn't sound very posh. What do the humans eat?'

'This is the food the humans don't eat,' the waiter explained. 'We serve whatever they drop on the floor.'

'I wonder what the Tinby would eat,' Sandra said. 'If it had a mouth, I mean.'

But the Tinby was not at the table.

MOUSE NOSES ON TOAST

WHILE PAUL AND SANDRA WERE DECIDING WHAT TO order, the Tinby had made a decision of its own. It would find out what humans ate for a posh meal and ensure its friends had the same.

Tinbys are skilful climbers, and this Tinby was one of the best. By the time Paul and Sandra stepped out from under the charming antique dresser, it was already halfway up the leg of the nearest table.

'There it is!' Sandra cried, pointing at the small checked shape. 'We must do something.'

But they could only stand and watch.

At last, the Tinby flipped itself up onto the tabletop, where it leapt for safety behind a salt-and-pepper pot and stood very still, blinking its small black eyes.

'I think it wants us to follow,' Paul said.

The Tinby had had a change of plan. Rather than bring the food to its hungry friends, and have to carry a dinner plate down a table leg without spilling, it would lead its friends to the food.

But how would Paul and Sandra reach the tabletop?

Not even a mouse can climb a varnished table leg, and Sandra's hands were made of tinfoil.

As the man paid the bill, the Tinby looked at what was left of his meal. Where you or I would see a plate of half-eaten spaghetti, the Tinby saw an opportunity. Before the waiter had time to remove the plate, it tied together five spaghetti strands and dangled them over the edge of the table.

Paul and Sandra did not like this, not one bit. What if the spaghetti snapped? What if the knots became undone? What if they got tomato sauce on their fingers?

Paul sighed. 'We'd better do what the Tinby wants, or it will sulk.'

So the mouse and the Christmas-tree decoration climbed the clever pasta rope, Sandra going last so that she could laugh at Paul's blue bottom.

When they reached the top, there was no Tinby.

They were about to give up and climb

back down when the Tinby appeared from nowhere, like magic.

'It was here all along,' Sandra said. 'We couldn't see it, as it matches the tablecloth.'

Sandra was right. The Tinby and the tablecloth were patterned with the same yellow and lime-green check. All it had to do was close its small black eyes and it was invisible.

A married couple were shown to the table. Paul and Sandra hid behind the camouflaged Tinby, and watched closely. The married couple were rich. The man wore a silk tie with a gold tie clip, and the diamond on the lady's wedding ring was as big as Paul's head.

But the real shock came when they ordered their meal.

'I will have the colourful parrot soup,' the lady said, 'with extra beaky bits.'

'And I,' said her husband, 'will have mouse noses on toast.'

The waiter flipped open his notebook and wrote this down. 'Would that be with whiskers, sir, or without?'

The man thought about this.

From his hiding place behind the Tinby, Paul thought about it too. He thought about his mouse friends under the floorboards in the storeroom. Were they running around without noses?

Surely humans didn't eat mouse noses on toast? Perhaps Paul's nose was poking out from behind the Tinby, and the rich man could see it, and had invented the meal as a joke?

But no.

A minute later, the waiter returned with a silver tray and placed two plates on the table. And there, on one of the plates, was a slice of toast, and on the slice of toast were half a dozen little brown noses.

TINBY TROUBLE

THE TINBY WAS COOL, SO COOL THAT IT SOMETIMES smelt of mint. It took a lot for the Tinby to lose its cool, but something about the plate of mouse noses on toast pushed it over the edge.

Before Paul and Sandra could stop it, the Tinby was on the toast, rolling in the butter and kicking the noses with its little square legs.

The lady cried out in horror. Her husband tried to grab it, but it ran up the silk tie and onto his head. The man leapt up from his chair and began waving his arms madly, trying to knock the Tinby from his hair, but the Tinby was nimble and would step out of the way with split-second timing.

Some customers carried on eating as though nothing had happened. Others decided that the man was under attack from a swarm of bees, and ran to the toilet to hide.

The waiter tried to help by hitting the man on the head with a French loaf, but this made him even more frantic, and gave the Tinby a chance to escape. It ran up the side of the French loaf and somersaulted onto the top of the charming antique dresser, where it disappeared into the dust.

Bertrand Violin, the restaurant manager, came out of the kitchen to see what the fuss was about. Bertrand was an old man with a bad back. His back was so bad he was bent almost double, and could only look at tabletops and shoes.

With no Tinby to hide them, Paul and Sandra had crouched behind a small silver bowl. As Bertrand made his way through the restaurant, Paul and Sandra began to fear for their lives.

'Quick! In here!' Sandra cried. They lifted the lid from the silver bowl and climbed inside.

The sides of the bowl were decorated with a pattern of tiny holes. Paul put his eye to one of the holes and peered out.

Bertrand Violin was studying the rich man's tie. He knew a lot about ties, and could tell that this tie ought to be plain, not covered in buttery footprints. 'What has happened?' he said, holding the tie to his tongue.

'Mr Violin,' the waiter said, 'we did have a minor incident with an overgrown bug, but it has been dealt with, I assure you.'

The rich man was so timid that this would have been the end of it, buttery tie or no buttery tie, but his wife had other ideas. 'Demand an apology,' she said, jabbing him in the ribs with the diamond wedding ring.

'My wife demands an apology!'

'Demand compensation,' yelled the rich woman, unscrewing the ring from her finger, 'or this ring goes in the soup!'

'Sir, madam,' Bertrand Violin said gently, 'please return to your chairs. This matter will be dealt with, you have my word.'

'We don't want your word,' the rich lady said. 'We want dinner free of charge. And a double helping of pudding.'

'Certainly,' Bertrand said, leading them back to their chairs. 'Waiter! A bottle of champagne, on the house.'

Inside the silver bowl, Paul and Sandra began to wonder what they were lying on. It was dry and powdery, and smelt of unwashed socks.

'It's cheese,' Sandra whispered. 'We're inside a bowl of parmesan cheese!'

'My bottom will be purple,' Paul whispered back. 'If we don't get out of here soon, it will fall off, and I won't have anything to sit on.'

Outside the bowl, the rich married couple were discussing what had happened. 'It looked like an insect,' the man said. 'A huge yellow beetle, with exotic lime-green markings.'

'We should call the health inspector, have the place closed down,' his wife said. 'It's unhygienic. And look at that!'

'What, dear wife?'

'A rat's tail, poking out of the silver bowl.'

'How odd,' the man said. 'It's in the shape of a question mark.'

'Stab it with a fork.'

The man picked up a fork and lifted the lid.

 # THE RESCUE

NOTHING COULD PREPARE PAUL AND SANDRA FOR THE terrifying experience that was to come. The world was torn from beneath them, and their brains were sent hurtling to heaven.

What actually happened was this. Rowley Barker Hobbs had grown tired of waiting for his bone, and had scampered round to the rear of the restaurant, where he entered the backyard through a gap in the fence.

He had expected the backyard to be like his overgrown garden at home, but filled with hundreds of bones. It would be raining bones, and bones would grow on trees. Imagine his disappointment when he found himself in a narrow concrete passage, with several rubbish bins at one end and not a bone in sight.

He was pleased to see Paul Mouse standing on the lid of one of the bins, wearing sandals and a pair of sunglasses. When he looked more closely he saw that it wasn't Paul at all. He said hello anyway, as he was Rowley Barker Hobbs.

The mouse lifted his sunglasses. 'Who are you?'

'Rowley Barker Hobbs,' said Rowley Barker Hobbs.

'Larry,' the mouse said, holding out a paw.

The paw was too small for Rowley Barker Hobbs to shake, so he lay on his back instead, to show Larry Mouse his tummy.

'That's a nice tummy,' Larry said. 'Tell me, Mr Hobbs. Do you live in this building, by any chance?'

Rowley Barker Hobbs shook his head.

'I was hoping you could show me around. I'm looking for some friends of mine. Mouses. Do you know where they might hang out?'

Rowley Barker Hobbs did not know, but he knew how to chase his tail, so he did.

'If you help me find them,' Larry said, hopping onto the dog's back, 'I will buy you a bone.'

A bone? The very word made his tail wag.

Perhaps the bone would be magic. Yes, it was a magic bone that grew bigger with each lick, bigger and bigger and bigger, until the whole world was one giant bone with Rowley Barker Hobbs sat on top.

The thought of a magic bone sent Rowley Barker Hobbs racing around the yard, knocking over the rubbish bins and saying hello. Larry Mouse had to grip the fur tight or he would fall off.

The chef opened the back door to see what all the noise was. Rowley Barker Hobbs knocked him flying, and raced through the kitchen to the dining area, where he said so many hellos that several customers spilt their food and several fell off their seats.

Just as Paul and Sandra were quivering under the approaching fork, Rowley Barker Hobbs ran into the rich man, who stood up too quickly and flipped the table over with his knee. The silver bowl soared across the room and hit the far wall with a clang.

Paul and Sandra tumbled out, and landed on the dessert trolley, where they bounced on a strawberry jelly and sploshed into a tasty peach-and-cherry trifle.

'We're alive!' Paul said as they climbed out.

'Just about,' Sandra said, wiping trifle from her eyes. 'What happened?'

'Rowley Barker Hobbs happened,' Paul said.

The restaurant was in chaos. None of the customers were eating now. Several had walked out. The dog was still circling the tables, the chef chasing him with a rolling pin.

Rowley Barker Hobbs only calmed down when he saw his two friends. He skipped up to the dessert trolley and gave them each a hello lick, swallowing the trifle in one gulp.

THE SAVAGE

PAUL AND SANDRA WERE HELPED ONTO THE DOG'S BACK by a mouse they had never seen before, a hippy mouse in sunglasses and sandals. They might have lost their Tinby, but Rowley Barker Hobbs had found them a new mouse friend.

Out on the pavement, Paul bent over so Sandra could examine his bottom. It had turned the brightest shade of electric blue.

'Is it bad?' Paul asked anxiously. He was already upset after losing his cape and hat in the trifle.

'No,' Sandra said, rubbing her bruised wings.

'It looks awful from where I'm standing,' Larry said.

This made Paul cross. 'Who asked you anyway?'

'Take no notice of Paul,' Sandra said. She introduced herself, and asked Larry his name.

'Larry,' the hippy mouse said, shaking her tin-foil hand. He held out a paw for Paul, but Paul refused to shake it.

'Paul is allergic to cheese,' Sandra explained. 'It makes his bottom turn blue.'

'The fur falls out too,' Paul said, 'and my tail curls up like a question mark.'

'I know a cure for cheese allergies,' Larry said. 'I will tell you later. First, you have to shake my paw.'

Paul apologised for being rude and shook Larry's paw. There was something about this mouse he hated, but if Larry knew a cure for cheese allergies, Paul Mouse was all ears.

'You two wait here with Mr Hobbs,' Larry said. 'I have to answer a call of nature.'

On one side of the restaurant was an area of wasteland where an old wooden house had once stood, and this was where Larry went for a pee. He had just found a suitable place when a strange creature leapt out of the brambles and began dancing around him in a circle.

Larry ran.

'That was quick,' Sandra said when he reached his friends.

'You've peed all down your leg,' Paul chuckled.

But something was wrong. Larry was so out of breath he could only stand and point.

Sandra put her arm round him, and led him to a shaggy armchair paw.

'I was attacked by a savage,' Larry said at last. 'I'm lucky to be alive.'

'What did it look like?' Paul asked, suddenly concerned.

'Like a pack of playing cards on legs,' Larry explained. 'Its chest was covered in medals. I thought it was going to eat me.'

'I think we should investigate,' Sandra said, 'don't you, Paul?'

Paul nodded. As long as the savage didn't throw cheese at them, he was ready for anything.

MORE TINBY TROUBLE

PAUL, LARRY AND SANDRA LEFT ROWLEY BARKER HOBBS on the pavement and ducked through a gap in the brambles. The plan was to approach from the opposite direction and take the savage by surprise.

'I don't like this place,' Sandra said. 'It gives me the creeps.'

'It gets worse,' said Paul, who had explored the area before. 'Where the old wooden house used to be, that is where the rats live.'

Mouses hate rats. Christmas-tree decorations don't like them much either.

'It happened just over there,' Larry said, pointing nervously.

'Then we need to head left,' Paul whispered. 'This path curves round to the right, straight into rat territory.'

So they took a path off to the left.

This was a mistake. It wasn't long before the brambles met overhead, then closed in all around them until they found themselves in a dead end.

When they turned round, they saw the savage. It had been following them, its little square legs picking silently through the undergrowth.

Larry's fur stood on end.

Paul and Sandra recognised it immediately as the Tinby, their Tinby, who lived with them in the shoebox at the bottom of Rowley Barker Hobbs' garden. But there was a coldness in its eyes, as though it viewed them through a thick sheet of glass.

As for the medals, this was stranger still. After they had left the restaurant, the Tinby had returned to the rich couple's table, grabbed the mouse noses from the toast and stuck them across its front.

Paul stepped forward to say hi, but the Tinby jumped back, startled.

'That's not like the Tinby,' Sandra said. 'Tinbys aren't afraid of anything, and we're its friends.'

This was news to Larry. 'You know this creature?'

'We did,' Sandra said.

Larry was confused, so Paul and Sandra explained what had happened.

They told him about the trip to the Mouse Restaurant, by the far wall of the human restaurant,

under the charming antique dresser.

They explained how the mouse waiter had offered them food that the humans had dropped on the floor, and how the Tinby had gone in search of something posh.

Then they told Larry how one of the humans had ordered mouse noses on toast, a meal so horrific that the Tinby had gone insane.

'I have heard of mouse noses on toast,' Larry said. 'A delicacy, like caviar. I thought it was a myth.'

When they rejoined Rowley Barker Hobbs on the pavement, the Tinby didn't follow. It was a wild thing now, and would live alone in the brambles, guarding its medals and dancing its mad Tinby dance.

'I'm sorry, Mr Hobbs,' Larry said as the padded nose came down to say hello. 'Not only did I not get you that bone, but we've lost your Tinby.' He turned to Paul and said, 'I promised Mr Hobbs a bone if he would help find my friends. They live in the restaurant somewhere, but I don't know where.'

'Mouses?'

'Cheese addicts,' Larry said. 'Graham Mouse is always on the Old Stilton, if I remember, and Mazie

42

and Suzie use cream cheese as fur conditioner.'

'You know Graham, and the twins?'

'We lived together in a cupboard in the old wooden house,' Larry said, 'just before it was pulled down. They moved into the restaurant with lots of other mouses, but I stayed on in protest. I tied myself to the plumbing with a piece of string.'

Paul laughed.

'It may seem funny to you,' Larry said, 'but some of us stand up for our beliefs.'

'But the building was pulled down,' Paul said.

Larry looked at the pavement, ashamed. 'When I heard the bulldozers I got scared, and paid a rat to gnaw through the string. That was three years ago, and I haven't seen the other mouses since.'

OLD FILTH

OLD FRIENDS

GRAHAM AND THE TWINS HAD THOUGHT LARRY MOUSE had died in the wreckage. Imagine their surprise when his sunglasses dropped through a gap in the floorboards, followed by one of his sandals, and then Larry himself, who landed on his head with a painful thud.

'Larry!'

The twins, Suzie and Mazie, hugged him warmly. Graham Mouse patted him on the back.

'How did you find us?' Suzie asked, handing Larry a thimble of freshly squeezed cheese juice.

'Paul brought me here,' Larry said, putting on his sunglasses. 'He has a blue bottom!'

Larry's other sandal hit Larry on the head. 'Ouch!'

'That was a secret,' Paul said, poking his nose through the floorboards.

'Paul is allergic to cheese,' Larry explained. 'It makes his bottom turn blue.'

'The fur falls out too,' Paul said, 'and my tail curls up like a question mark.'

'Is that why you wear that fashionable suit?'

45

Mazie asked.

Paul nodded. 'It's also why I'm not coming down.'

'You have to come down,' Larry told him. 'I'm calling a meeting.'

Graham folded his tattooed arms. 'Don't tell me you're organising another protest.'

'Not a protest,' Larry said. 'A campaign.'

Up in the dusty storeroom, Sandra was trying to persuade Paul to go down. 'You can't hide your blue bottom forever.'

'All right,' Paul said, 'but before I go down, you have to hide all the cheese.'

Sandra agreed, and when Paul arrived five minutes later there was not a crumb of cheese in sight.

 # THE MEETING

Twenty-three mouses lived under those floorboards, and even those Larry had never met knew of his brave attempt at stopping the bulldozers. The idea of a campaign caused quite a stir.

Larry Mouse stepped up onto a matchbox and raised his paw. The mouses and the Christmas-tree decoration gathered round, and the meeting began.

'We all know that humans have disgusting eating habits,' Larry said dramatically.

'Get on with it!' Graham shouted, and several other mouses laughed out loud.

Larry stepped down from the matchbox. He would not get on with it, not until each mouse was quiet.

'I think everyone had better listen,' Sandra whispered, 'or we'll be here all day.'

Graham nodded. 'The next mouse to interrupt Larry gets a punch on the ears.'

Larry Mouse was back up on the matchbox. 'Where was I? Yes, we all know that humans have disgusting eating habits, but there is one human meal that can only be described as sickening, and that meal is mouse noses on toast.'

'Myth!' one of the mouses shouted.

Graham looked round, and the mouse fell silent.

'Not only do humans eat mouse noses on toast,' Larry went on, 'but they pay a lot of money for it. To humans, mouse noses are a delicacy.'

'Myth!' another of the mouses shouted.

Graham said nothing.

'Mouse noses on toast are a myth,' the first mouse said, stepping forward, 'like caviar, and colourful parrot soup with extra beaky bits.'

'I swear on my blue bottom,' Paul said, taking Larry's place on the matchbox, 'mouse noses on toast are real.'

'We saw it with our own eyes,' Sandra said.

'I didn't see it myself,' Larry said, 'but when we left the restaurant I went for a pee in the brambles.'

He tried to tell them about the Tinby, how it wore the noses on its chest like medals, but the mouses were in hysterics.

'Larry went for a pee!' they shouted. 'Paul has a blue bottom!'

'There's nothing wrong with taking a pee,' Larry

said. 'I bet there isn't a mouse in this room who hasn't peed at least once today.'

'Mouse noses on toast!' the mouses shouted. 'Caviar! Myth!'

Larry was about to give up when something small and brown plopped through a gap in the floorboards and landed on Graham's head.

It was a mouse nose.

'Yuck,' Graham said, holding the little brown thing in his paw.

'That,' one of the twins said, 'is the most disgusting thing ever.'

Larry stepped back onto the matchbox. This time when he spoke, the mouses listened.

TROUBLE IN THE STOREROOM

AFTER THE MEETING, PAUL AND SANDRA CLIMBED UP through the gap in the floorboards where the Tinby had thrown the nose. The Tinby was no longer there, but it had left some interesting clues.

'Footprints,' Sandra said, pointing to a trail of square markings in the dust. 'And look. Another mouse nose.'

'The footprints lead over to the window,' Paul said. They climbed onto the window ledge and looked out.

They could see Rowley Barker Hobbs waiting patiently in the street. Paul tapped on the glass and the shaggy sheepdog came bounding up to the window, saying hello to the glass with his paws.

'If we can get this window open, Rowley Barker Hobbs can come in,' Sandra said.

'Locked,' Paul said, examining the latch. 'The Tinby may still be in this room.'

'We should look for it,' Sandra said. 'It may need our help.'

The walls of the storeroom were lined with shelves. The shelf nearest the window held a long cardboard

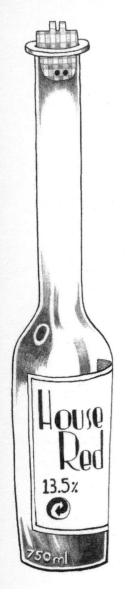

box, and this was where they began their search.

Paul gnawed a tiny hole in the side of the box with his teeth. 'Cabbage,' he sniffed, poking his nose through the hole.

'The Tinby hates cabbage,' Sandra said. 'Let's try another.'

The box beside that contained dried herbs, and the one beside that was empty. Up on the next shelf they found a box of candles and a large sack of flour. On the next shelf were two rows of cooking oil, and higher up still was a huge box of cheese, with a hole in the side where the mouses had helped themselves.

And high, high up on the top shelf they found the Tinby. Somehow it had become wedged in the neck of an empty wine bottle, upside down.

'It looks distressed,' Sandra said.

'I wonder why it climbed in there,'

Paul said, scratching his ears. 'Perhaps it thinks it's a cork.'

Actually the Tinby thought it was a spaceship, but that was not why it was in the bottle. It had seen something horrible and had squeezed into the bottle to hide.

Paul climbed the rough brickwork, put one paw on the neck of the bottle and peered inside. 'Can you hear me?' he called, and the Tinby wriggled its little square legs in reply.

'We'll never get it out,' Sandra said. 'The poor thing is stuck fast.'

'We need something slippery,' Paul said. 'Washing-up liquid should do it.'

But Sandra had a better idea. With one shove, she sent the bottle sailing over the edge of the shelf.

For a brief moment, the Tinby was moving faster than any Tinby had moved in the entire history of the world. Then, SMASH, the bottle shattered into a million silver-green stars.

By the time Paul reached the floorboards, the Tinby had gone, leaving only a Tinby-shaped mark in the dust.

Paul called for Sandra to come down, but she

refused. 'I think you should come back up,' she said. 'And bring Larry with you. I have found something he may find interesting.'

THE PROTEST

FURTHER ALONG THE TOP SHELF, IN A DARK AND DUSTY corner, Sandra had found a box marked MOUSE NOSES WHISKERS ON. The top was open, but the box lay on its side and some of the noses had spilled out.

Paul was stood with his paw on his hips, knee-deep in noses. Graham was there too. Larry had stayed under the floorboards. He had important work to do, he said, organising the campaign.

'We should take some down for Larry,' Graham said.

'No,' Sandra said, 'I have a better idea.'

A minute later, Larry looked up to see a huge sheet of cardboard drop through the floorboards. The words MOUSE NOSES WHISKERS ON were printed across it in big letters. Larry was halfway through reading the word ON when a second sheet of cardboard landed on his head.

'They're flaps,' Paul said.

'From a cardboard box,' Graham added.

'Graham tore them off with his bare paws,' Sandra said.

'A box?' Larry said, scratching his ears. 'A box of noses?'

The second cardboard flap was blank on both sides. Graham ripped it into several cardboard squares, and Sandra glued a matchstick to each square to make them into signs. Larry wrote a message on each with a huge felt-tip pen. HANDS OFF OUR NOSES, read one. MOUSE NOSES SMELL, read another.

'That one doesn't make sense,' Paul said.

'It's a double meaning,' Larry explained. 'What's the old joke about the dog with no nose?'

The twins knew the joke, and told it together.

'My dog has no nose.'

'How does it smell?'

'Terrible!'

Paul looked at the sign. 'It still doesn't make sense.'

The plan was to protest in the restaurant itself, to make the customer think twice before ordering mouse noses on toast. Everyone agreed that this was a good plan, but it did have one flaw. If the chef caught them, he would chop them up with a knife.

Paul shook his head. 'I don't like the sound of this.'

Larry picked up his sign. JUST BECAUSE WE

SQUEAK, it read, DOESN'T MEAN WE'RE MEEK.

'Look,' he said, 'can we just get on with it? There are mouses having their noses cut off this very moment.'

Larry could be very persuasive at times, and this was one of those times. When he marched out of the dusty storeroom that warm afternoon, his sign held high above his head, the mouses followed.

It is rare to see twenty-five mouses and a Christmas-tree decoration marching across the floor of a posh restaurant, chanting protest songs and waving cardboard signs. The customers carried on eating at first, not believing their eyes. Then, when they realised that the mouses were real, the restaurant erupted as customers ran screaming from the room.

For Sandra and the mouses it was as though the sky was falling in, as stilettos, shoes and boots crashed down all around.

'Back to the storeroom!' Larry yelled.

They didn't need telling twice.

WHAT NOW?

'THAT WAS A DISASTER,' PAUL SAID, SHAKING HIS SORRY EARS.

Sandra and the mouses were sprawled out in the mousehole, under the dusty storeroom. Sandra was trying to straighten her halo, which had become buckled in the stampede.

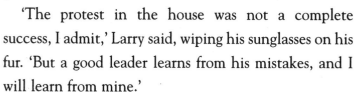

'A disaster?' Larry said, standing up. 'It all went perfectly to plan.'

Graham laughed. 'Just like your protest in the old wooden house!'

'The protest in the house was not a complete success, I admit,' Larry said, wiping his sunglasses on his fur. 'But a good leader learns from his mistakes, and I will learn from mine.'

'Then learn from this one,' Graham said, 'and cancel the campaign.'

Larry was dumbstruck. 'Cancel the campaign? Graham, do you realise what happened up there? We emptied the restaurant. Some of those customers will never return. A few more demonstrations like that and mouse noses on toast will be taken off the menu, for good.'

'If you think we're going back up there,' Paul said, 'you're crazy.'

Larry was pacing the room, stepping over his exhausted friends. 'Losers. That's what you lot are. Losers.'

'I'm a loser all right,' Paul said. 'A loser with a blue bottom, and bruises all the way up his tail.'

'At least you still have your nose,' Larry said. 'Unlike thousands of other mouses, standing noseless in some nose-removal factory.'

Larry paused for effect, then continued.

'Noses in boxes, noses in the back of a truck, noses on toast. Noses gurgling about in a horrible human tummy. It's enough to make you sick.'

No one said anything to this. What could they say? Larry was right, and only a mouse with an apple pip for a heart could hear his words and not feel moved.

Larry leant against the wall, scratching his ears in thought. 'What we need now,' he said, 'is Direct Action. We strike, and we strike hard.'

'How do you mean?' Paul said, standing up.

'If they want noses, we give them noses. More noses than they can stomach!'

THE MOST PATIENT DOG IN THE WORLD

THEY HAD THE NOSES, A HUGE BOXFUL. THE PROBLEM was how to transport them to the room above the dining area without being seen.

'We set up a system of pulleys,' one of the mouses suggested. 'Out the storeroom window, up, and in.'

'Too complicated,' Larry said.

'I could carry them up,' Graham said, flexing his muscles.

'Too heavy,' Larry said.

'We throw them up the stairs one at a time,' one of the twins suggested.

'Too tiring,' Larry said.

'We eat them,' the other twin said, 'scamper up the stairs, and be sick.'

'Too disgusting,' Larry said.

The youngest of the mouses, a tiny, squeaky mouse named Inch, thought they should use magic.

'Too impossible,' Larry said.

'We tie the whiskers together to form a mouse-nose snake,' Paul said, 'and drag them up.'

'Too stupid,' Larry said.

'We build a time machine,' said a mouse who had watched too much Cheddar Television, 'and travel to a time in the future when the problem has been solved.'

'Too idiotic,' Larry said.

It was Sandra who came up with the best idea. 'All we need to do,' she said cleverly, 'is give the dog a bone. We buy Rowley Barker Hobbs a bone as a present, and he will carry the noses for us.'

There was one problem. They didn't have any money, and you can't buy a bone without money, not even in a story.

'Where is Rowley Barker Hobbs?' Larry asked.

'Out on the pavement,' Paul replied.

'He's been waiting out there all this time?'

Paul nodded. He knew Rowley Barker Hobbs like the back of his paw, and he knew that the shaggy sheepdog would never wander off without saying hello.

'It seems to me,' Larry said, 'that Rowley Barker Hobbs is the most patient dog in the world. I suggest we write him an IOU and buy the bone later.'

'What's an IOU?' squeaked Inch.

'An IOU is a piece of paper which means I owe you

something,' Larry explained. 'The something is whatever is written on the piece of paper.'

'Or drawn on the piece of paper,' Sandra said. 'Rowley Barker Hobbs can't read.'

The next problem was how to lower the box of noses to the storeroom floor. They needed string, and they had none.

It was Graham who solved this problem. He emptied the noses onto the shelf and sent the cardboard box sailing down to the dusty storeroom floor, just as Sandra had done with the wine bottle. They only had to shove the noses off the shelf and they would land in the box with a soggy plop.

While this was going on, Sandra set about unlocking the window. She did this by bending her halo into the shape of a key. Rowley Barker Hobbs said hello to the glass with his paws. The window swung open and in he leapt, wagging his happy tail.

'Mr Hobbs,' said Larry, the only mouse who had remained on the storeroom floor, 'we have a bone for you. Well, a picture of a bone. The real bone comes later. First, we need your help.'

'Why aren't you shoving noses?' Paul said, tapping

Larry on the shoulder.

'Someone has to keep an eye on the box,' Larry replied, and Paul had to admit, he had a point. 'What about you, Paul? Why aren't you shoving noses?'

'I was shoving noses,' Paul said. 'I just came down to find out why you aren't shoving noses.'

Graham had come down too. He stepped out from behind Paul and gave Larry an army salute. 'Noses shoved, sir.'

'Right,' Larry said, clapping his paws. 'Are you ready, Mr Hobbs?'

Rowley Barker Hobbs was always ready. That was what being the most patient dog in the world was all about.

LARRY THE COWARD

WITH NO STRING TO SECURE THE BOX, THE TWENTY-FIVE mouses had to ride on Rowley Barker Hobbs' back and hold it steady with their paws. Sandra perched on his padded nose, to shout directions. The stairs were steep and rickety, which made the ride bumpy, especially for Inch. He had forgotten to take his travel-sickness pills and turned a queasy shade of green.

Not even Larry knew what they would find when they reached the top. Perhaps the home of Bertrand Violin and his elderly wife, Bertranda. Or the chef, who sharpened his knife in the dark, and cut off the nose of anyone who dared visit.

But the upstairs rooms were empty.

The room above the dining area had no windows, and was lit only by the light that shone up through gaps in the floorboards.

There was only one customer in the restaurant now, a huge man with a bald head. If the man had looked up, he would have seen Larry's eye peering through a mouse-sized hole in the ceiling.

The waiter flipped open his notebook, took a pencil from behind his ear, and walked up to the man's table.

'Six slices of mouse noses on toast,' the man said, licking his lips. 'Three with whiskers, three without.'

Larry stood up. 'Right,' he said, clapping his paws. 'I need a volunteer.'

Silence.

'A volunteer, brave as a lion, to sacrifice his or her nose to save the noses of mouses for generations to come.'

Paul raised his paw, but not to volunteer. He had a question. 'What does the volunteer have to do?'

'Plug the hole,' Larry said, pointing to the hole in the floorboards. 'We pour the noses over the plugged hole. When I give the signal, we yank the plug by the tail. Up comes the plug, down go the noses.'

'You've got a fat head,' Paul said, 'why don't you plug the hole?'

'I have to give the signal.'

'I could give the signal,' Paul said helpfully.

'My sandals would fall off,' Larry said.

Paul laughed. Larry, he decided, was a coward.

'What did you mean,' one of the twins asked, 'when

you said the volunteer would sacrifice his or her nose?'

'Figure of speech,' Larry said.

The twins were not convinced, and did not volunteer. Neither did Graham or any of the other adult mouses. The only mouse to volunteer was Inch, the smallest, squeakiest mouse of all.

'You're too small,' Larry said. 'You would slip right through.'

'I could wear my jumper,' Inch squeaked. 'My nan knitted it for my birthday.'

The jumper was red, and as thick as a thick slice of cheese. The mouse who fetched it from the storeroom had trouble carrying it up the stairs.

'This is a thick jumper,' Larry said, feeling the wool.

'Nan doesn't want me to catch cold,' Inch squeaked, pulling the jumper over his ears. 'Which way do I go? Downside up or upside down?'

'Upside up,' Sandra said.

Inch squeaked a startled squeak. 'I don't want noses on my head.'

'Then plug the hole upside down,' Larry said.

Climbing into that hole was the hardest thing Inch had ever had to do, apart from sums. It would be scary enough for a human, but Inch was a tiny mouse. To Inch, the room below looked as big as outer space.

When the noses piled on, Inch almost squeaked his last squeak. If you have ever had your rude parts sniffed by two thousand tiny nostrils, you will know how he felt.

Hurry up and pull my tail, Inch thought.

But Larry had a problem. To give the signal he had to look through the hole. How could he look through the hole when it was plugged by a mouse?

'You should have thought of that,' Paul said, 'before you sent poor Inch into that hole.'

'I hope he's all right,' Sandra said.

'Are you all right in there, Inch?' Larry called.

'No!' came the tiny, squeaky reply. 'The noses have gone down my jumper. The whiskers are tickling my tum!'

'Inch, can you see a huge man with a bald head, eating six plates of mouse noses on toast?'

'Yes!' came the tiny reply. 'Unplug me quick, I need

a wee!'

'We'd better get him out of there,' Sandra said.

'There's too many noses,' Larry said. 'I can't see his tail.'

'Then get in there and find it!'

Larry was horrified. 'Me?'

Graham gave him a mean look, and he knew the game was up. He had to prove he was brave, or the mouses would never squeak to him again.

DIRECT ACTION!

GRAHAM WAS STOOD AT THE EDGE OF THE NOSE PILE, calling Larry's name.

'You'd better go in and get him,' Sandra said, chewing her halo nervously. 'You're his best friend.'

'Best friend my spanner,' Graham said, and in he went.

Any second now, Sandra thought, Graham will come leaping out, dragging Larry by the ear. But another minute passed with no sign of Graham or Larry.

'You two go in there,' Sandra said to the twins. 'He's your friend too.'

Suzie and Mazie kissed each other goodbye and in they went.

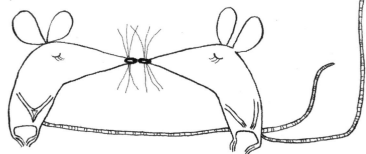

The twins won't get lost, Sandra thought. Mazie will look after Suzie and Suzie will look after Mazie. But two minutes later there was no sign of either.

Sandra turned to Paul. 'I know you two don't get along,' she said, 'but you would miss him if he wasn't around.'

Paul took a deep breath and dived in.

A minute later another mouse disappeared into the nose pile, followed by another and another until there were no mouses left, just a silver Christmas-tree decoration and a dog with a happy, happy tail.

'Perhaps you could help,' Sandra said.

Rowley Barker Hobbs gave the noses a sniff to check they weren't a new type of bone, and shook his shaggy head.

'Well I can't go in there,' Sandra said. 'I'm an angel, and drowning in noses is not very angelic. We'd better call the police.'

But when they reached the bottom of the stairs, something soggy happened.

Mouse noses are wet, like dog noses. If you want to pile them up on old wooden floorboards you had better dry them out first, or the floorboards will rot and the noses will fall through.

This is bad enough, but if your nose pile contains twenty-five mouses without parachutes, you have a disaster on your paws.

As the huge bald man bit into his sixth slice of mouse noses on toast, he heard an awful sound. The sound of soggy wood splintering. The sound of a thousand noses slipping through a soggy, splintery hole. The sound of twenty-five mouses screaming in terror.

SPLEAURAAAAAAAGH!

From the bottom of the stairs, all Sandra and Rowley Barker Hobbs heard were the painful cries of the huge bald man. They raced in to find him flat on his back on the tiles, covered from head to shoe in soggy, sniffy noses.

The mouses had a soft landing. This was a man who had eaten six slices of mouse noses on toast every day for ten years, and that was just for starters.

He would follow the mouse noses on toast with a piping hot bowl of colourful parrot soup with extra beaky bits, a platter of deep-fried ostrich feet and a broad blue elephant-ear omelette, with a giraffe's neck on a spit for main course and a bowl of stripy-bee sweets for dessert.

The chef heard the noise too. He was on the toilet reading a cookery book, and by the time he had pulled up his trousers and dashed through to the restaurant, the mouses had scarpered.

THE PETITION

'I'VE HAD ENOUGH OF THIS,' PAUL MOUSE SAID, pouring a thimble of water over his head. 'I'm going home.'

'Me too,' Graham said.

'Graham, you are home,' Larry said, drying his sunglasses on a mouse towel. 'You can't go home if you're home already.'

'Don't tell me what to do,' Graham said angrily. 'I'll box your big ears!'

The mouses were in the mouse bathroom, washing off the icky sticky noses. The bathroom had been made by gnawing a hole in a pipe. Water dripped into an old tin bathtub with the words REFORMED HAM printed on the side.

'My jumper smells of bogies,' Inch squeaked.

'Jumpers can be washed, Inch,' Sandra said, patting the tiny mouse on the nose. 'No one was seriously hurt, that's the main thing.'

'Stop complaining,' Larry said. 'The Direct Action went perfectly to plan.'

Paul shook his head. 'But at what cost? Look at poor Inch. He's terrified.'

'I'm ferry tied,' said Inch, who had trouble with any word longer than his tail.

But Larry wouldn't listen. 'Right,' he said, clapping his paws. 'Where do we strike next?'

'We've had enough Direct Action for one day,' Sandra said. 'How about we try something sensible? We could stand in the street and ask people to sign a petition.'

Everyone agreed that this was a good idea, and ten minutes later they were all stood out on the pavement.

The streets were deserted. The only human to pass by was an old lady.

'Excuse me!' squeaked the mouses, 'will you sign our petition?'

The old lady didn't even look down.

'This is hopeless,' Larry said. 'Where is everybody?'

'Rowley Barker Hobbs has figured it out,' Sandra said. 'Look!'

They all looked.

'He's peeing up a lamppost,' Larry said.

Halfway up the lamppost, someone had fixed a

wooden sign, with a picture of the Prime Minister and an arrow pointing up the street.

'Of course!' Paul said. 'Today is the day the Prime Minister comes to town. The arrow points to the Town Hall, where the Prime Minister gives his Big Speech.'

Larry clapped his paws excitedly. 'Let's get some more signatures and take the petition to the Town Hall. If we hurry, we can present it to the Prime Minister in person.'

'How many do we need?' Sandra asked.

'One hundred,' Larry said. 'You always need one hundred. It's the law.'

'And how many do we have?'

Larry looked at the sheet of paper. 'None.'

'We could sign it,' Paul said. 'How many would that be, Sandra?'

Sandra counted. There were the twenty-three mouses who lived under the storeroom, and Larry and Paul, which made twenty-five. Then there was Sandra herself, and Rowley Barker Hobbs, and Rowley Barker Hobbs' nose, and Rowley Barker Hobbs' tail, and Rowley Barker Hobbs' four paws, which added up to thirty-three.

'Close enough,' Larry said. 'We can get a few more on the way.'

THE PRIME MINISTER

LARGE CROWDS ARE VERY FRIGHTENING FOR TWENTY-FIVE mouses and a Christmas-tree decoration, especially when their taxi keeps jumping up at people.

'I wish Rowley Barker Hobbs would stop saying hello,' Paul said as they neared the Town Hall.

'Mr Hobbs!' Larry yelled. 'Keep your paws on the pavement, or we will fall off!'

Rowley Barker Hobbs was a multilingual dog and could say hello in three different languages: jumping-up language, licking language and tail-wagging language.

'Stick with tail-wagging language for now,' Sandra said, perching on Rowley Barker Hobbs' nose.

'How about licking language?' Rowley Barker Hobbs said, licking a woman's hand.

'The sooner we reach the Town Hall,' Sandra whispered in the woolly ear, 'the sooner we get you that bone.'

There is nothing like the thought of a bone to keep a dog on the right track, and soon enough they reached the Town Hall gates, where hundreds of tourists were taking photographs of the back of a policeman's head.

Being tiny is hopeless most of the time, but it can come in handy. Sandra and the mouses were able to run under the gates and through the Town Hall door without getting arrested or squished.

The Prime Minister was in a posh office, rehearsing his speech. 'Intonation, intonation, intonation,' he muttered to himself. 'Must work on my intonation.'

When he looked down at the posh desk he saw a mouse wearing sunglasses and sandals. 'I like your suit,' the mouse said. 'The purple tie matches your nose.'

The Prime Minister didn't say anything. He wasn't used to being squeaked at.

'Allow me to introduce myself,' the mouse said, bowing low. 'My name is Larry Mouse. I represent a group of pet-sized political extremists, the MADAMNOTs. Mouses, Angels and Dogs Against Mouse Noses On Toast.'

The Prime Minister just stared. Had he been working too hard? Was he seeing things?

'We have travelled many meters by paw-power to bring you this petition,' the mouse said. He held out a sheet of paper, black with paw prints. 'If you

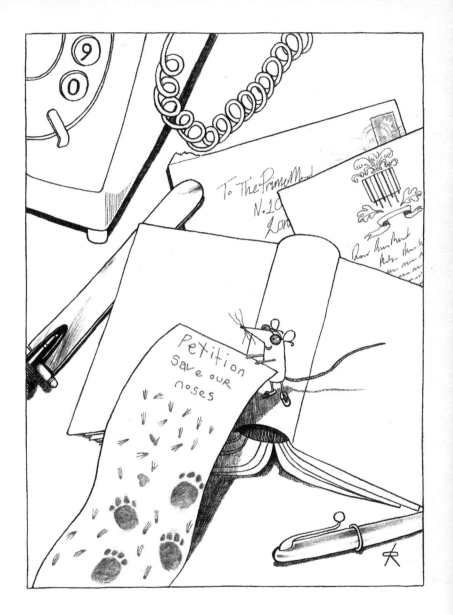

would consider–'

Before the mouse could squeak another squeak, the Prime Minister's bodyguard whacked him across the room with a broom.

The Larry who returned to his friends in the corridor was an ashamed sort of Larry, with a red bottom.

'You've got a red bottom,' Paul said, pointing rudely.

'No I haven't.'

Paul was in hysterics. 'Your bottom is redder than mine is blue. Are you allergic to something?'

Larry nodded. 'High-speed brooms.'

'So what happened?' asked Graham. 'Did you give the Prime Minister the petition?'

Larry thought about this. If he told the truth, they would think he was a failure.

'Larry,' Sandra said firmly, 'did you or did you not give the Prime Minister the petition?'

'Yes,' Larry said shiftily. 'In fact, yes.'

'And what did he say?'

'He vowed to introduce a ban on nose-based food products,' Larry said. 'He's going to announce the new law tonight, in his Big Speech.'

'Then we'd better find a seat,' Sandra said. 'I

wouldn't miss this for the world.'

Larry was less keen. 'Can we go home? I fancy a big lump of cheese.'

'I smell a rat,' Paul said, giving Larry a sniff. 'We should hear what the Prime Minister has to say. If Larry is telling the truth, this could be an historic mouse moment.'

THE PRIME MINISTER'S SPEECH

THE ATMOSPHERE WAS ELECTRIC. THE HALL WAS PACKED with politicians, journalists, TV cameras and members of the Royal Family. One of the most powerful men in the world, the Prime Minister of Great Britain, was about to give his Big Speech.

Larry and Paul had the best seats in the house, on the Prime Minister's shoes. Sandra and the other mouses watched from the side of the stage, hidden among the folds of the velvet curtain. Inch was so excited he wet himself.

At last, the Prime Minister gripped the podium with his hands and cleared his throat.

To Larry, the speech seemed to go on for hours. Every few minutes, Paul would ask him when the Prime Minister would start talking about mouse noses on toast. 'Any minute now,' Larry would say, his paws crossed behind his back.

Just as the Prime Minister was about to unveil his new food policy, something plopped onto the shoulder of his suit. It was brown, and had whiskers.

'The Tinby!' cried Sandra, clapping her silver hands.

If the viewers at home had watched closely, they would have seen a Christmas-tree decoration dash across the stage, where it ran behind the podium and hopped aboard the Prime Minister's left shoe.

'Paul, Larry,' cried Sandra, 'did you see what happened?'

'Not from down here,' Paul said.

'All I can see,' Larry said, 'is the Prime Minister's hairy nostrils.'

Together they climbed the Prime Minister's suit and leapt onto the podium. From here, hidden among the microphones and wires, they could see across the entire hall. And the first thing they saw was a mouse nose, plopping onto the top of the Prime Minister's head.

When he looked up, another mouse nose hit him in the eye, splat!

'A direct hit!' said Paul. 'Where are they coming from?'

'The Tinby must be up in the roof,' Sandra said.

The Prime Minister

had barely uttered a word when a fourth mouse nose hit him in the other eye, splat! He stumbled blindly away from the podium, catching his suit on a nail. The nail pulled his trousers down, revealing a pair of red, white and blue boxer shorts.

Several posh people fainted, and one of the Prime Minister's biggest supporters dropped his flag and began to cry. Most people just laughed, but not for long.

Up in the ceiling, the Tinby was leaping from rafter to rafter, spraying the room with icky, sticky noses.

Tinbys can be lightning-fast, and this Tinby was the fastest in the business. Within minutes, every person in the hall was covered from head to shoe. Where the Tinby had got so many noses I do not know. Perhaps it had bought them mail-order, and paid for them with a yellow and lime-green checked cheque.

The Prime Minister had to be led from the stage by bodyguards. The police were called, but were too afraid to enter the building. The army were called, but they were afraid too, so the army sergeant called the SAS, who stormed the building with machine guns, firing randomly at the ceiling.

No one was hurt, but several people were treated for shock, and the Royal Family had to have their jewellery cleaned by experts.

THE PRIME MOUSE MINISTER

Up in the rafters, Sandra and the mouses could find no sign of the Tinby.

'I hope the SAS didn't shoot it,' Sandra said. 'It could be lying dead, full of bullets.'

'Tinbys are far too busy to waste time getting shot,' Paul said. 'Even mad Tinbys.'

Larry shook his head. 'I doubt the Tinby is mad at all. What could be more sensible than throwing noses at the Prime Minister?'

'But what about all those people?' Sandra said, gazing down at the terrible mess the Tinby had made of the hall. 'They didn't deserve to have noses thrown at them. I bet they don't all eat mouse noses on toast. Some may even be vegetarian.'

'And besides,' Paul said, 'whatever your politics, that was no way to treat a Prime Minister.'

'Indeed.'

Paul span round. On the next rafter stood a mouse in a smart suit.

'I,' the mouse said grandly, 'am the Prime Mouse

Minister. I was here to give my annual Small Speech, but after what happened, I don't think I'll bother.'

'I don't blame you,' Paul said. 'I'm Paul, and this is Sandra and Larry, and this is Graham and the twins.'

'Never mind the introductions,' the Prime Mouse Minister said. 'Who was that creature? I thought it was a bar of soap, till it started throwing noses.'

'That,' Larry said, hopping onto the Prime Mouse Minister's rafter, 'was the Tinby.' And he told the Prime Mouse Minister all that had happened, and about their political work as the MADAMNOTs, Mouses, Angels and Dogs Against Mouse Noses On Toast.

The Prime Mouse Minister was impressed. 'Nothing could be more abhorrent than a plate of mouse noses on toast. Alas, no Prime Minister could publicly support a group of terrorists, but off the record I wish you the best of luck.'

'We're not terrorists,' Sandra said. 'This is a peaceful campaign.'

'It doesn't look peaceful to me,' the Prime Mouse Minister said.

'The Tinby isn't a MADAMNOT,' Sandra said. 'Mad, yes. MADAMNOT, no.'

'Peaceful protest can only achieve so much,' the Prime Mouse Minister said. 'Your bar of soap has the right idea. If the campaign is to bear fruit, you may have to take a more, shall we say, direct approach.'

'Direct Action!' Larry said with a cheesy grin.

THE RAID!

Mouses are not thieves. The only thing mouses steal is cheese, which isn't really theft as mouses secretly own all the cheese in the world.

But the mouses were on a special mission.

On Larry's orders, Suzie and Mazie scampered into a human clothes shop and stole three pairs of woolly gloves.

The SAS wear black woolly hats pulled down to cover their faces, with a hole for each eye. Larry explained that these were called balaclavas, and that mouse balaclavas were made from woolly gloves, by gnawing off the tips of the fingers and poking eyeholes with a stick.

Sandra chose not to wear one, as balaclavas are not very angelic.

'Shouldn't they be black?' Graham said, pulling his balaclava over his ears.

'Pink is in fashion,' Mazie said.

The Mouse Nose Abattoir was on the edge of town, surrounded by forest. The Four-Legged Terrorist

Transportation Unit stopped behind the safety of a tree stump, and Sandra and the mouses climbed down.

'I recognise that building,' Paul said.

'Me too,' Sandra said. 'It used to be a shoe shop. It was where the Tinby found the shoebox we call home.'

Where the words BOB'S SHOES had been, it now said MOUSE NOSE ABATTOIR in black plastic letters.

'This building,' Larry said dramatically, 'is the most evil building on earth. To the right you can see a line of mouses queuing by a huge human door. Inside, the mouses are taken into a dark room, where they hear a terrible snipping sound. SNIP!'

Inch covered his ears with his paws.

'What happens to the other parts of the mouse I do not know,' Larry said, 'but the noses are packed into boxes, carried out the back and loaded onto a huge truck.'

'Why don't the mouses run away?' asked Paul.

'They've been brainwashed. They think they're here to test a new type of cheese.'

'How do you know all this? Have you been inside?'

Larry shook his head. 'I hear rumours, Paul. I have big ears.'

'So what's the plan?' Sandra said.

'Plan?'

'I have a plan,' Paul said. 'We forget the whole thing and go home.'

'This is no time for homely thoughts,' Larry said. 'If you need courage, think of the millions of mouses who have lost their noses. To those noseless mouses, a lump of cheese is as odourless as a stone.'

Beneath his pink balaclava, Paul blushed bright red.

Suzie had a plan too. 'The easiest way into a building is through the door. We wait for the door to open, climb aboard the Four-Legged Terrorist Transportation Unit, and we're in!'

'I was about to think of that myself,' Larry said.

The hardest part was the wait. What would they find inside? Humans with knives? Or a denosing machine with metal teeth?

They were about to find out. The huge door swung open and in walked the first brainwashed mouse.

Larry clapped his paws. 'This is it, MADAMNOTs. Victory is but a whisker away!'

THE MOUSE
NOSE ABATTOIR

ROWLEY BARKER HOBBS HAD NEVER BEEN A
Four-Legged Terrorist Transportation Unit before. He
was very excited. The moment Sandra and the mouses
were aboard, he was through the door in one happy leap.

The door slammed closed, missing his tail by inches.
Inside, he bounced about the abattoir full speed, saying
hello to anything that stood in his path.

'Slow down!' Larry yelled. 'You'll get us all killed!'

But Rowley Barker Hobbs was saying hello too
loudly to hear.

'We have to make a jump for it,' Larry said to Sandra
and the other mouses. 'Abandon dog!'

They tumbled to the floor, and landed in a confused,
furry heap.

'Watch out for the
knives!' Larry cried, and buried
his nose in his paws.

But the knives never came.

A mouse approached, a friendly
mouse with a pencil behind his ear.

'What's all this about?'

'We're here to rescue you,' Larry said. 'Let's get out of here, before the humans cut off our noses.'

The mouse just laughed. 'No humans in here. If a human entered this building, we'd be out of business in a squeak.'

'I don't understand.'

'This isn't really an abattoir,' the mouse explained, helping Larry to his feet. 'This is a nose factory, run entirely by mouses. I'm the Foremouse. This is Annie Mouse, my assistant.'

'You mean the noses aren't real?' Larry said, taking off his balaclava.

'We make them out of marzipan,' the Foremouse said.

Annie Mouse adjusted her glasses and read some words from her clipboard. 'Marzipan is a paste made from sugar, almonds and eggs. Humans use it to decorate cakes.'

'Put on these white coats,' the Foremouse said, 'and we will show you around. Your shaggy friend will have to wait here. They don't make mouse coats in dog size.'

'Sorry, Mr Hobbs,' Larry said, patting Rowley Barker

Hobbs on the paw.

The Foremouse led Sandra and the mouses through a second huge human door. The door was opened by fifty stunt mouses in crash helmets, who stood on each other's heads to form a daring mouse tower.

'Clever,' Paul said with a nod.

'That's just the start,' the Foremouse said.

The back room was bustling with hundreds of busy mouses in white coats.

'This tub is full of marzipan,' Annie Mouse said, lifting the lid from a plastic tub and scooping some out with her paw. 'Taste it.'

'It looks like soft cheese,' Paul said.

'Wow!' cried Inch. 'It tastes like sweets.'

'These mouses are forming the marzipan into nose shapes,' Annie Mouse explained. 'We could shape the noses by machine, but to fool the humans every nose must be different.'

'Are these the brainwashed mouses we saw queuing outside?' Larry asked.

The Foremouse laughed. 'The mouses aren't brainwashed. Our workers are paid in good quality Cheddar.'

'Over here,' Annie Mouse said, 'the noses are placed on a conveyor belt which carries them to the painting area.'

She led them to where several hundred mouses were sat at tables, painting the marzipan noses with mouse paintbrushes.

'We use a special paint made of snot and brown food colouring. The snot gives the noses a snotty, nosey taste.'

Inch chuckled.

'And over here we add the finishing touch, the whiskers,' Annie Mouse said. 'Some humans like their noses with whiskers, some like their noses without.'

'How do you make them sniffy and soggy?' Inch asked.

'Simple,' Annie Mouse said. 'We leave them out in the rain.'

'This factory is amazing,' Larry said.

'Thank you,' the Foremouse said proudly. 'We talk to the humans on the telephone. That happens up here.'

They all scampered up a shoebox stairway, up onto the huge wooden desk where the old shoe-shop owner used to do his accounts.

A mouse was shouting into a microphone. The mouse was butch, and had a deep voice, more of a rasp than a squeak. A cable led from the microphone to a loudspeaker, where the voice could be heard as loud as a human voice. Another group of mouses held a mobile phone to the loudspeaker with their paws.

'The order will be ready at twelve o'clock tonight!' the mouse shouted. 'Not a moment before!'

'Do the humans pay for the noses with human money?' Sandra asked.

'That is the cleverest part of all,' Annie Mouse said, leading them through another huge door. 'We told the humans that the factory is owned by a fat millionaire who loves cheese. The humans pay us in fresh Cheddar!'

CHEDDAR MOUNTAIN

THE LAST ROOM CONTAINED THE BIGGEST, PONGIEST, cheesiest pile of cheese you could ever imagine. It smelt as though five hundred netball players had taken off their shoes and socks and wriggled their cheesy toes.

It was a pong all right. The sort of pong that mouses like!

'This,' Annie Mouse said proudly, 'is Cheddar Mountain.'

Sandra and the mouses just stared. Paul had never seen anything this scary in all his life. If this didn't make his bottom fall off, nothing would.

Every few minutes, a mouse would take off its white coat and scamper to the top of the mountain, its ears almost touching the ceiling, and stuff its greedy mouth with cheese.

'Help yourselves,' the Foremouse said. 'There's plenty to go round.'

Inch wriggled out of his coat without even undoing the buttons, and up he went.

'Hold my flip-flops,' Larry said, passing them to

Sandra. 'I may be some time.' And he went up the mountain too.

Then followed Graham and the twins, and then all the others, until the only mouse left was Paul.

The Foremouse gave him an odd look. 'What's wrong? Don't tell me you don't like cheese?'

'I have a cheese allergy,' Paul said sadly. 'It makes my bottom turn blue, and my tail curl up like a question mark.'

'Your bottom is already blue,' the Foremouse said, looking at Paul's bottom. 'And your tail couldn't get any curlier.'

'Paul,' Sandra said, 'I think you should climb Cheddar Mountain. What have you got to lose?'

Sandra was right.

Was it really so bad having a blue bottom, and a tail that looked like it wanted to ask you something?

Paul took a deep breath and scampered to the top of Cheddar Mountain.

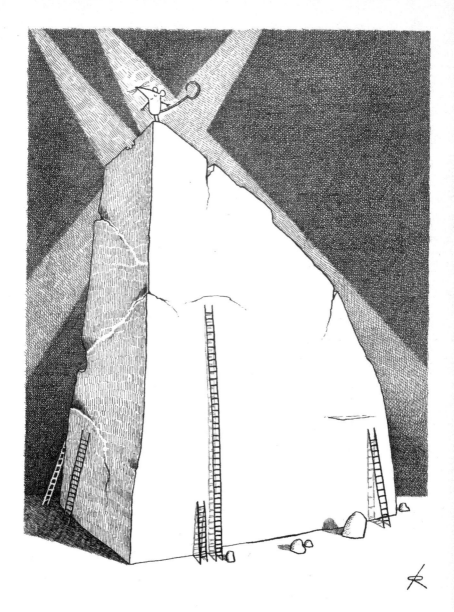